Published by Hachette Partworks Ltd.
ISBN: 978-1-906965-14-3
Date of Printing: November 2012
Printed in Malaysia by Tien Wah Press

THE ARISTOCATS

Disney

hachette

Once upon a time in the city of Paris, France, there lived an elegant lady called Madame Bonfamille who lived in a grand mansion with her four cats.

Their names were Duchess, a beautiful white creature, and her kittens Marie, Toulouse and Berlioz. Madame loved them more than anything in the world. They were her Aristocats.

The kittens were a talented threesome. Toulouse loved to paint.

Marie, on the other hand, preferred to sing...

...while Berlioz accompanied her on the piano.

Edgar, the butler, also lived in Madame's mansion. Edgar secretly hated her little companions. He loathed tidying up after them, preparing their meals and most of all, tying their pretty collar ribbons every day.

One day, Madame dressed up to look her best because she was expecting a special guest, the lawyer George Hautecourt, her dearest and oldest friend. She wanted to draw up a will. She had already decided who would inherit her riches.

"I would like everything to go to my beloved cats as long as they live," she declared. "Then, when they're gone, my entire fortune will go to Edgar."

The butler, who had been eavesdropping, couldn't believe his ears: "I have to come second to those cats?!" he spluttered.

Edgar was furious. Those cats would have to go!
So he embarked on an evil scheme. First, he
mixed some sleeping tablets with their favourite
food. Once the cats were asleep, he would take them
somewhere far, far away. They would never find
their way home and the inheritance would be his!

When the butler brought them the tasty "crème de la crème à la Edgar" the pussycats lapped it up delightedly: it tasted wonderful!

The first part of Edgar's wicked plan worked like a dream. In no time, everyone was fast asleep!

As soon as it was dark, Edgar placed the
slumbering Duchess and her kittens in a basket
and crept out into the moonlit night.

No one saw the butler put the basket of
cats into the sidecar of his motorcycle, start
up the motor and set off for the countryside.
Everything was going according to plan.
Until he happened upon two guard dogs who
did not like the noise of his motorcycle.

They chased him off of the road, and
the motorcycle hit a bump. The basket
containing Duchess and her kittens flew
out of the motorcycle, falling safely by the
side of the river.

Soon after, Duchess and the kittens awoke. Where were they? Who had taken them there, to such a dark, cold place?

The dismayed kittens cuddled up to each other in the basket. Duchess thought sadly about poor Madame. "She'll be so worried when she discovers we've gone!" she sighed.

At last, that awful night drew to a close. As dawn broke, Thomas O'Malley, a cheerful alley cat, was strolling along the river. As he sang a cheery song, he spied Duchess on the opposite bank. She was exquisite! O'Malley decided to introduce himself. Duchess seemed quite fascinated with her strange new friend.

Duchess asked O'Malley if he could tell her the way back to Paris. Meanwhile, one by one, the kittens crept out of the basket to get a better look at this rather un-aristocratic cat. They'd never met a cat like him before!

Thomas O'Malley kindly offered to help them.

"Leave it to Thomas O'Malley. We'll fly to Paris on a magic carpet!" he declared, leaping onto the branch of a tree.

The magic carpet O'Malley had in mind turned out to be a passing milk van. As it trundled along the road, O'Malley fearlessly jumped onto the bonnet, startling the poor milkman so much that he slammed on the brakes.

O'Malley quickly guided
the Aristocats into the back
of the van. "All aboard for
Paris!" he called.

But before they could get to Paris, the cats had
to leap off the van in a hurry. The angry milkman
had caught them having their breakfast – the fresh
cream he was about to deliver!

Luckily, they soon found the road for Paris!

The five cats soon reached some railway tracks and decided to follow them into the city.

After a while, the tracks crossed a river on a bridge. "Look at this great bridge! Come on, let's play trains!" said Toulouse to the other kittens.

But as they tiptoed along the rail, they suddenly realised that a train was speeding towards them!

Quick as a flash, the cats dived for cover under
the track. The huge train rattled past inches above
their heads, making a terrifying noise. Toulouse and
Berlioz trembled with fright, and poor little Marie
lost her balance and fell into the river!

O'Malley dived to the rescue, even though, like all cats, he hated water.

"Hold on Marie, I'm coming!" he yelled.

Struggling against the strong current, O'Malley managed to grab Marie.

O'Malley swam over
to Duchess who had
climbed a large
overhanging
branch.
With one
outstretched
paw, she
caught hold of the
petrified kitten!

Duchess and her kittens
had found a true friend.
Soon, their protector led
them into the heart of his
beloved city: Paris!

By now, night had fallen and the full moon cast a magical glow over the rooftops of the city. But not even Marie, who was usually very romantic, took much interest in the view.

"Mum, I'm tired!" she complained. O'Malley kindly offered her a piggyback.

They were all tired. But clever Thomas O'Malley knew somewhere safe where they could rest.

O'Malley's safe place turned
out to be an attic with an old
bed and some rickety furniture.
And as for resting... forget it!
Scat-Cat, an old friend of
O'Malley, was busy tooting
his trumpet with his band of
musical jazz-cats. They had
turned the dingy attic into a
swinging dance club!

O'Malley introduced Duchess and her family to Scat-Cat's band. O'Malley and Scat-Cat started to dance...

... then the excited kittens joined in...

... and finally even the ladylike Duchess couldn't resist the beat, and agreed to dance with O'Malley!

It was now the middle of the night, but Thomas O'Malley and Duchess had important things to talk about. They had realised how much they cared for each other, and O'Malley wanted Duchess and her kittens to stay with him for good.

But Duchess decided
that they must return to
Madame. The kittens, who had
overheard the conversation,
sighed with disappointment.
"We almost got ourselves a
dad!" whispered Berlioz.

The next day, the Aristocats finally reached
Madame's home. While Duchess and O'Malley said
their goodbyes to one another, the kittens raced
happily towards the mansion and meowed loudly at
the front door. Edgar was horrified when he opened
it! He had been so sure that he'd got rid of the cats
for good.

As soon as the cats were inside, the butler
threw them into a sack.

Then, hearing Madame's voice, he locked them
in a trunk.

Edgar pushed the trunk out into the road. He was
going to load it onto a delivery van that was parked
outside the gate. He would send them to Africa.
There was no chance they could make their way
back from there!

But O'Malley, who had heard Duchess and the kittens meowing for help, rushed to their aid. He pounced on Edgar's back from behind.

Madame Bonfamille, hearing the commotion, rushed outside, calling: "Duchess! Kittens! Where are you? Come here!"

As soon as she saw her beloved pets in the trunk she realised what the butler had been up to. The cats hadn't vanished mysteriously, as he'd told her – he was responsible for their disappearance!

Madame ordered Edgar to leave at once and never come back.

At last she was reunited with her darling cats!

When she noticed O'Malley she cried out: "What a handsome fellow! Shall we keep him in the family?" The kittens meowed in approval.

And that's exactly what happened. Thomas
O'Malley was part of the Aristocat family now.
Together with Duchess, Toulouse, Marie and Berlioz
he posed for a family portrait.

Madame was overjoyed.

"Come on, my little treasures, get a bit closer!" the lady cried out cheerfully as she snapped the camera shutter. "Say cheese... and think of the delicious feast that's waiting for you all downstairs!"